THE FAULT

The Fault

poems

Marcela Sulak

BLACK LAWRENCE PRESS

Black Lawrence Press

Executive Editor: Diane Goettel
Cover Art: "Depth III" by Avital Cnaani
Book Cover and Interior Design: Zoe Norvell

ISBN: 978-1-62557-076-5

Published 2024 by Black Lawrence Press.
Printed in the United States.

CONTENTS

ACKNOWLEDGEMENTS

The author is grateful to the editors of the following journals for previously publishing poems from this collection, sometimes in slightly different forms or with different titles.

American Poetry Review: "The Fault," "Women, Immigrants, and
    Wages," and "Seed Bank"
The Cincinnati Review: "Tooth"
The Columbia Review: "Periodic Table of Elements"
DIAGRAM: "Feathers I & II," "To Listen One Must Love Seeds,"
    and "Sugar Fence Moon"
Hinchas de Poesía: "Tools"
Jet Fuel: "Frank Takes a Fence" and "The Boat Rocker's Post Script"
JuxtaProse: "Brazen," "Delight," and "Inalienable"
Laurel Review: "Wedding Gift"
Main Street Rag: "The Nest"
Miniskirt: "Granted"
The Nervous Breakdown: "The New Math"
Nine Mile Magazine: "Double Life" and "Spider"
Phantom Drift: "Rampart"
Pleiades: "Bed"
Poetry Northwest: "The Polishing of Stones"
Rogue Agent: "Storyboard"
Scoundrel Time: "Words Made Flesh"
Split Lip Magazine: "The Cost of Art"
SWWIM: "Naming the Animals"
Waxwing: "Show Your Work"
Zócalo Public Square: "The Voice"

I am grateful to the Virginia Center for the Creative Arts for a residency at Moulin à Nef in Auvillar, France, during which time some of this story was written.

Thank you for your incisive criticism and support, Julie Choffel, Alison Powell, Lisa L Moore, and Debora Kuan. Thank you to my Poem-a-Day-for-a-month writing communities—Sarah Wetzel, Nicole Callihan, Iris Jamahl Dunkle, Zoë Ryder White, Kimberly Nunes, Jane Medved, Maya Klein, and Karen Marron. Thanks Mama and Daddy for teaching me all the things. And most of all, I am grateful to my daughter, my greatest delight and most faithful compass, who shows me things as they are, and sometimes as they might be.

1.

SEED BANK

My parents could hardly get through breakfast
without mentioning sex. As in, *I told you
I had a cold last night, but you insisted*,

in lieu of *bless you* after my father sneezed.
We never invited any school friends over.
To love is to learn new habits, with holes in them,

for a vole or a mole, they too hunger, for a seed
or surprise— for example, an aboriginal grass
with exceptional nutritional value sold in hip

restaurants in capital cities at night, which
is how I discover decades later the weeds
in my garden were chicory. Meanwhile,

my father and brother discuss planting organic
—you can make a killing if you pitch it right
and if the insects, weeds, drought, and rain

don't mess up a crop. Life isn't a hobby,
after all. To love is to discern which fields
will become habitual, which words will turn over,

which pauses will yield sturdy seed banks,
which silences will reduce the water content
by 1% and which will reduce the temperature

in the room 10°F, for, taken together,
this will double the seed lifespan.
Which trees, for example, can be grafted

in such a way as to yield oranges, grapefruit,
lemons, and pomelos, all from a single trunk.
And which pecan trees can survive a watering

by the progeny with a gasoline can—he said
he was only trying to help, though, knowing him,
he was also trying for sparks, and for sparking

the pollinating flies, for love, it is so flighty a thing.

FEATHERS I

Rolled up in the top cupboard in Tel Aviv, tied with string and covered in a garbage bag is a flock of feathers. Feathers that once flew over blue pockets of water and fields gold with wild mustard, daisies, and dried grass. Feathers that once belonged to Canadian geese on their migrations between Canada and Mexico, or South Texas where they'd winter, filling the skies with their vees for weeks, the traffic of their wings and honks. They'd wake us in the morning, and they'd clutter the air every night. Geese my uncles shot half a century ago at least. And my grandmother and aunts plucked. Feathers my grandmother stuffed into a comforter.

I was so happy when I'd asked for and received it. I'd also requested the bread knife thin as the moon the geese passed over each November, but it was thrown away.

Inside the top cupboard are the feathers. I can feel them beating against the door. I can feel the comforter shift with their weight. And I don't know if it is the feathers or if it is my aunts or if it is the stitches of my grandmother, but that comforter is filled with nightmares. I have to air out the dreams for two weeks before I can sleep. Even Lorena, who came home with me for Christmas since she couldn't go home to Mexico for semester break, said, "Your grandmother was deeply unhappy when she made that comforter for you." "But that's the thing," I tell the feathers, rustling even now, for I will take them down when I am done writing, "you were not made for me."

DOUBLE LIFE

Walking home along the Yarkon River
I'm wondering what a decomposing human body looks like
at three months. It's odd
how there are no books for that, no *What to Expect When You've
Stopped Expecting*. What
is the inverse of *your baby is now the size of a grapefruit*?
I am this decomposition,
and at the same time, alive on the earth above.
And the dull pain of moving
my head from side to side, up and down, is exciting,
feels so good. I am dressing up
as a witch, and Maya, as a vampire, for Halloween: women
who aren't expected
to smile. We pretend they're only costumes. Every year I recall
my grandmother of blessed memory,
who complained that her nursing-home roommate, in a near-
vegetative state, was spoon-
fed every day, but my grandmother, who had to feed herself,
paid the same rent. I loved her

pleasure in complaining. My mother, who would answer
Grandmother's calls
and leave the phone for half an hour at a time to do the dishes
and laundry, then pick it back up
to say *uh huh* every now and then, always said my grandmother
delighted in complaining.
It was a joy to her. My body is here on earth, not composing

5

complaints with my grandmother's,
where, I am imagining, the worms and gasses would have parted
the bones eventually
and given the buried body a modicum of relief in an otherwise
afterworld of stillness,
because still I wake with pain if I lie in place too long.

How had I come to be crushed on the roadside like an animal?
Just as I'd begun to leave my life, and
I'd felt myself reaching for what comes next, I'd remembered
I had a daughter, and
my daughter became the nail on which the soul catches when reaching out,
and the helicopter blades
of the life-flight protested loudly through the spiritual air till any
angels would have had
to move out of the way or be sliced, I couldn't see out the window
to tell. And yet there is delight
where I can find it. Today it is the artichokes I patted
into the soil, whispering *grow,*
grow, it will be okay. And F's boyish body stabbing into mine
and holding my hand after,
and holding my arms in a shroud-like embrace until I always wake
and move somewhere else,
and even then no one lets me rest in peace, for he comes looking
for me to ask *what is it?*
and it wakes me again every time, and I don't have an answer
for what it is I am now.

IN THE BEGINNING

The man and the woman had lied about the same things on their dating profiles—that they were morning people, that they never smoked, and that it would take 3–5 dates to sleep with someone they really liked. They both said their homes were clean, "but could use a touch-up."

This morning the woman scrubbed the sink and counters and the stovetop, and when she went for a run, she saw the sea had also been cleaning—it had withdrawn farther than it had ever been before, and the sands were shimmering in the sun.

They both said they drank "sometimes," by which they meant at night; it signaled the time they could relax. That morning, the stellagama the woman has been watching had crawled a little farther on, beyond the sea rocks to the sand rocks near Sde Dov airstrip, and the squill's white bells had begun to pucker.

They had both dreamed of the other that night; he that they were on a plane, she that they were on a boat. The conflicts of their dramas were not insurmountable, and they were on the same team.

The woman notes the stellagama hasn't been alone for several months now. And the woman is happy for him, and for all the white-throated kingfishers, the common kingfishers, the wrynecks, the black-throated loons, the black-necked grebes, and all the Egyptian ducks, not to mention the two kinds of cuckoo, and the ever-present laughing dove.

SHOW YOUR WORK

When the clinical psychologist sent me his webpage and résumé, and suggested we explore a potential relationship, it reminded me of my sixth-grade algebra teacher, who used to deduct points for not showing my work. Were I to show you my work just now, for example, I'd tell you I'd just finished Carmen Boullosa's novella *Before* and had begun Mary Ruefle's *My Private Property*, which I read with half my brain still in *Before*. Though two weeks ago I'd read Ruefle's *On Imagination* with such delight that everything I thought for a week after was phrased in her syntax. And this, I'd imagine, is how I would approach the meeting with the clinical psychologist. With half a brain in the last story.

For, indeed, I'd begun *Before* last month in order to test out F's new beanbag for reading. Earlier that afternoon Amalia and I had blown enormous soap bubbles and played dominoes and badminton in the Yarkon Park with Sebastian and Delfine and their four daughters, Lana, Mia, Or, and the fourth one whose name I can't remember just because it's indecent to be able to remember all four every time you run into them, whom we'd met by chance.

After Shabbat I watched *Maleficent* again with my daughter. (The last time we watched it the battle scenes traumatized her.) And all the next morning I was thinking of red lipstick. F phoned when I told him not to come over. When I said, wow you must really hate talking on the phone if you'd rather jump on your bike and ride it here and then go back and it's now 10:20 p.m., he said phones were for Haifa and Tel Aviv—or Jerusalem and Tel Aviv—not for Tel Aviv and Tel Aviv. But then again, I thought, as I am showing my work, they are for covering the distance also between inside a bar and outside, between the two blocks, if you've passed the meeting place unintentionally.

I also looked up the words *badminton*, which I always spell *badmitten* to myself, and *Maleficent*, and I double-checked to make sure I was spelling *Boullosa* and *Ruefle* correctly, which I was.

In sixth-grade algebra, Ms. Lili (we didn't know what to call her as she'd just gotten divorced) would deduct 20 points from my grade. It wasn't that the answer came to me in a dream or by intuition. It's just that I preferred to do it in my head because I was always out of erasers. And one day I told her, look, you've been giving me 80s all year for not showing my work. And I've still got the highest grade in class. Who do you think I might be cheating from? Which may be why, instinctively, I don't want to get to know any clinical psychologists in an intimate manner.

After that Ms. Lili began to give me full marks, and also, I began to show my work.

THE TWIGS

Today is the day they formally
meet in the portico of the nest
and the male and the female
tell their twigs. Sometimes
the female is very surprised
that what she's been calling
a twig, the male has been
calling something else. A leaf,
a splatter pattern, a breeze, for
example, a sudden movement.
Structural integrity evaluation,
he cries, tossing out two of her
twigs. They are too pointy
and bright and might be
mistaken for darts or darting
butterflies. The male and the
female make a fest and each
guest brings a twig. The male
says, nice fastenings! He is
so shiny. The female needed
to sparkle her shoes. Yet he
hadn't needed everyone to have
brought a twig he said. I
have enough twigs of my
own outside my nest, and
if, he notes, I want I can
put them in the nest or I can

leave them in the leaves.
Replies the female, oh, but
I haven't any twigs besides.
How I do need those twigs the
guests brought. Especially
the ones that look like sudden
butterflies, splatter patterns, and
leaves. How much I needed
them. I did.

THE NEW MATH

Although Sharron Hass has warned that rationality is the enemy of generosity

sex four times in one week $\div$ our public argument at dinner $=$
sex two times $\mathbf{X}$, your *I want to see you* text one workday at noon.

My four birthday presents for your four kids $\div$ (your telling me when your mother's birthday was by telling me you'd bought flowers for her
$+$
the fact that you did so only because I asked you what you did that day)
$>$ your mother phoning me on my birthday to tell me that her gift to me would be a new pair of sunglasses $-$ your dislike of my current pair of sunglasses.

My paying your daughter for an hour of "language lessons" each week to bond with her $=$ your tutoring my daughter in the new math[1]

You are the perfect size for me $-$ (*although some may consider you too short* $\mathbf{X}$ getting the color of my eyes wrong when saying what you love about my face) $<$ *this is the love of my life* in your love letter to me.

you don't look fat, you just look like you don't care how you look in that bikini $<$ the butter you spread on the bread you toast for me and the jam your mother made, the coffee you made for me, although you showed me how to use the coffee machine myself.

---

1 The way they teach math in school is never the way the parents learned it.

Your driving and supplying the biking supplies $=$ my cooking and packing the picnic lunches $-$ the trails being too far above my skill level.

The flowers you bought me $-$ I had to ask you to do it $-$ I don't like white chrysanthemums that have been dyed blue $<$ the massage you gave me $-$ (I gave you one first $+$ I had to ask).

My rage and fury $-$ my ability to say *I'm sorry* $>$ your buying grapes from the store in the middle of the grape harvest in my orchard and vineyard.

My unexpressed anger at your chatting with the landlord of the Airbnb for an hour on my "birthday getaway weekend" last year (trip with your kids since it was also your visitation weekend) while I waited for you to drive us to the Sea of Galilee $\neq$ your rage at my feeling, but not expressing, rage.

But someone has to keep track, so even though I keep forgetting it happened, you keep bringing it up, and then I keep remembering that you are wrong.

Extra credit for it having been the Sea of Galilee, and when you thought I was drowning in it, you began to swim out to me, with my daughter's pink float (which I'd blown up), though I'd swum out into the middle of the lake under those treacherous wind conditions in the first place just to get away from you.

THE BOUNDARIES

I spent an inordinate amount of time yesterday playing
with my boundaries, giving them baths, drying their fur,
giving them names and nuts.

What do you do when you find yourself in this situation,
I ask Sharron Hass, who is great with the zinger.
My boundaries are always asking

for her to come over and play. They call her Auntie Sharron.
I never find myself in this situation, she says.
I simply don't do situations.

F says that that was actually a good one-liner, this morning
when I tell him about my resolve to spend more time
with the boundaries.

I've just brought him some kale I sautéed with garlic
and ginger, sesame oil, because kale is the only thing
that grows in my garden that he'll eat.

It's actually all that grows right now, that and
passion fruit. And F doesn't like passion fruit either,
because of the texture.

Do you like caviar? I ask, and he says no,
because it's too salty. I tell him if he thinks
caviar is salty, it's a good thing

he doesn't love men. He tells me I should put that idea
in one of these poems, because boundaries,
they'll eat anything.

BRAZEN

Sure, I could just say *f*ck it, common caper is close enough*, for the name of this flower F sent me a photo of from his morning bike tour, thinking he would be sharing beauty with me and not existential angst, because no field guide in the world would allow that it's supposed to be in bloom right now.

I could say *f*ck it* to the fact I've been paying thousands of shekels a year for English classes, and my kid still can't remember how to spell "any," and I made her feel so bad she's just given me her savings jar with a note taped on it: *her is 200 and somting sheckuls it can pay for food cloths ene ting.* And the note made me feel even worse. Not for the feeling of guilt that prompted her to write it, but that she fucking misspelled almost every word in it.

The caper was included in ancient lists of items that could not be destroyed. It was called *brazen*, like the compulsion to curse, I guess. Or at least to write curses. I don't actually say out loud half the stuff I write. In *Tractate Beitzah 25b* we see *There are three who are brazen: Israel among the nations, the dog among animals, and the rooster among birds, and some also say the goat among small cattle, and some also say the caper among the trees.*

On his bike tour F did not lose his phone, misplace his credit card, crash his bike and break his ribs, or really anything of note, like he usually does. And it's driving me nuts, the name of that plant, that and my kid's inability to practice French horn though I pay 550 NIS a month (this is a discount because the French horn is "rare" and to be encouraged) and an extra 85 NIS a month for rental.

And I think you could create a new heaven and earth from discarded waste—money, food, irresponsible capers who are blooming out of season (*f*ck them*), and all the misspelled words and incorrect math formulas and the hours spent on the phone begging math tutors not to quit.

And let it be inhabited by the brazen with their pure white petals *spread like the wings of the butterfly* and the brazen hot pink stamens and their filaments, and the 350 species, which are 349 more than I have time to deal with today.

WORDS MADE FLESH

I am reading about a two-hundred-and-forty-seven-year-old document
found in the buttocks of a statue of Jesus in the Cathedral of Burgos
after restorers removed a piece of fabric used to cover Christ's
behind when J says she is perplexed by her extreme repulsion
        to her pre-adolescent son.

He "accidentally" cupped and squeezed her breast.
She screamed at him and pushed him. I tell her that once I
involuntarily (not-involuntarily) hit my child, pushing her hand
away from some-part-I've-forgotten-which of my body.
        The world is a weird place,

you never know how other people are going to interpret
your actions, better my kid learn that now. But all this time,
I've been thinking of the two pages written in careful calligraphy
with which I've casually covered J's breast, like that sheer paper
        a nurse places over your body

before a pap smear, because Jesus, if he is anything, isn't he the word
made flesh, so it makes sense that my orifices and J's protrusions are kind
of like the two-hundred-and-forty-seven-year-old note
written in calligraphy by a priest and stuck up the Savior's backside
        in the Cathedral of Burgos,

and that, when touched the right way,
could reveal time capsules of hurt deposited by those who came
before us. Because it felt so good, not to apologize to my daugh-
ter. Although, in the priest Joaquín Mínguez's case, it was a
pleasure chest. I don't remember which particular manuscript

my daughter had pulled out of me that day. But
I also remember feeling relieved that it was gone. And if
someone ever does it to you, you do to them exactly what I did to
you right now, I said. Here is a pen and ink and a crevice. You
know what I mean.

2.

DELIGHT

The truly awful thing about delight is that it can't be found only in the self, but needs the world to rub against. In fact, it depends exactly on not having what is external to you but wanting it very much. To have delight was introduced into English by the French, and it meant to desire, *avoir envie*.

The golden flowers blooming by the sea right now give me hay fever, for they delight in my nose. And allergies are the pollen thinking your nose is a flower and making flower love inside it with the intent to bear fruit. Though Hilla says she eliminated those symptoms of hay fever when she gave up eating dairy. Of course Hilla also gave up coffee, so she might just be stuck in the delirious hem between dreams and waking life. Her current delight is of the 15th century English variety—*pleasure, joy, or gratification felt in a high degree*. Specifically, her greatest and most transporting pleasure right now comes from having her head cradled by her herbalist's warm fingers for ten minutes. She feels complete. I suppose to feel complete is to fit inside something else.

Delight might be the word for the urge to gorge, the urge, when parting from my lover, to cut off his hands and tongue and cock, stuff them inside my various emptinesses all day until I suffocate, as in having a mouth that, when full, is already starving for the next bite.

I wanted to be saved, which is why I began to think about delight in the first place. I was seduced by the spelling, thinking it was light, only to discover that it was, in fact, the knife.

The etymological *delite* has generally been supplanted by *delight*, an erroneous spelling after *light, flight*, etc. Delight was, in fact, the opposite kind of pleasure than what I felt today, panting on rollerblades along the boardwalk, past the defunct electricity station, alongside the municipal airport that serves only two airlines, the planes bouncing on the tarmac, over the water, over the lizards sunning on rocks, the tortoises and sea turtles.

We are all after erroneous light, too, and I am skating, uphill against the wind, on one side of me, planes taking off and landing; on the other side, boats and paragliders plunging and lifting as sea turned into air, and me, stopping, turning, to be blown all the way back to where I'd begun, a soul rehearsing death, or a pre-soul rehearsing life, and nobody, no body whatsoever, the lightest bliss of all.

TO LISTEN ONE MUST LOVE SEEDS.

To listen one must love seeds.
Or, to love, one must listen to seeds. I forget.
This morning on the bridge across the ancient mills,

the cart driver collecting the garbage stopped to count
the courting cattle egrets. He was crooning
their vital statistics to his shadowed assistant.

The egrets were fluffing their feathers, and
editing the stats. To listen to this morning
is to love seeds. To pull the pole beans, pop

the casings, line the pockets. Every day I gaze
upon the scales of the anona, fruited away
in the canopy of my orchard, and every day

the anona grow plumper, taking their time,
un-anxious to please me. The oranges in their nets
don't orange. They are enjoying their green phase.

The seed banks of the world change places—the one
in Syria moves to Iraq. The one in Norway
begins to lend out seeds and then to collect.

There are gun banks buried underground—one
in Texas—these are called caches. When you dig guns up
they grow and grow. To love bodies, one must scratch holes

and listen to seeds. These. This morning picking beans,
my shoe slipped into a pocket of air. It was
a cache of vole. To love voles one must hunger,

muster hunger, desire darker ways of seeing,
seed the dark, and must love ceding.

FEATHERS II

I can't wait to go to sleep each night since F and I had sex on top of my grandmother's feather comforter the first night I got it down, aired it out, and laid it on the bed. My dreams have been spectacular—not a single nightmare among them. They are not my own dreams, of course, just as the nightmares the comforter used to bring hadn't been mine. Which makes them even better. Last night I was in Mexico in the mountains—chocolaty red earth and bronze shrubs lining the cutbacks. Close enough to the Texas border for there to have been a Czech koláč and Christmas decorations, a gas station and diner. The night before, my daughter was my sister and my mother sent us off to camp.

One night I dreamt I was a kite. My dreams remind me of Mary Ruefle's essay "Snow," in which the narrator opines that everyone should celebrate the first snow of the season by having sex with someone. She herself advocates the same partner every year, even if you both eventually marry other people. She imagines being in a classroom, noting the snowflakes, and announcing to her students, "Class dismissed, children. It is snowing. I must now go and have sex."

In the case of my grandmother's feather comforter, I must reevaluate my image of my paternal grandmother, an immigrant with a scar on her cheek from her brother's hatchet (she'd been standing behind him as he was chopping wood) and a fourth-grade education. You wouldn't notice unless she pointed it out—it blended with her laugh lines. I am sorry she is dead.

My grandmother's house had been decorated like a Habsburg estate—two sets of silver, dark furniture, a formal sitting room, and the walls hung with scenes of the Austrian Alps or blond gorgeous saints looking particularly virginal against dark backgrounds, clasping crosses or rosaries to their breasts and gazing at the viewer with tears in their eyes to inspire feelings of remorse. Maybe, like the wrathful feathers and ancient sorrow of my grandmother's feather comforter, or Mary Ruefle's snow, they were simply lacking a certain sex offering and that made them very sad. Especially galling, then must have been the usual platitudes and prayers directed at them instead.

One night I dreamt I was running across the savannah, gallivanting with giraffes and zebras, as if I'd stepped into one of those National Geographic children's puzzles. One night I dreamt I was a smooth beige stone skipping across the surface of a pond.

I made such pretty ripples.

MY LIFE ON EARTH WITH MALLOW AND ANGELS

Four months after the accident I ran two miles and climbed three locked gates, only to fall from my lemon tree. I also hauled a wheelbarrow of dirt. Iman, a new mother, shared her recipe for mallow and onions. Mallow are weeds I tear from my garden, but they are young and tender now. They require much cleaning, are good for milk production.

Last night F and I met for a beer and talked about our encounters with ghosts. Mine were actual, and F's were from books and the woman he once instantaneously fell in love with. My cousin's colleague, a teacher who grew up near us, says she was named for the ghost of their house when I'd asked her about her unusual and beautiful name. It was also my classmate's name. I wonder if she was named for the same ghost.

F hadn't shaved because I'd told him I liked stubble, but then he'd worked from home that day. We kissed because he was beautiful in his body like that. And on Sunday I got lost among the angels of the households of Mea She'arim and walked among them, like a ghost, watching them buy candies and lotto tickets and cello tape and books and onions in their own natural environment, one of them even had a run in her hose. I

didn't fit in—I had no lipstick. And then we descended
bit by bit far below the ground, and the train took us
faster than we ever believed possible, ducking us again
and again under the waves of mountains, the threads
of mallow roots emerging in the sun, just long enough
to catch our breath.

THE NEST

after Heather Christle

This place is our nest now.
Behave as if you were
in a nest. I said these things
to the man as soon as he got
home. The man looked at me
and at the little nest, and he
said to me, M, he said,
in this nest, you have
your egg, and I have mine.
There is no need, said
the man, to put our eggs in
the same basket. I begged
the man not to mix
metaphors. He should keep
his metaphor on his side
of the nest, and I would
keep mine on my side.
How then, the man asked
me, does one live in a nest?
A nest, I answered, is
an orchestra of spontaneity. Please
put aside the hammer and the
tape measure and bite
yourself a twig, I said. Before
I moved into his nest, the man

had often spontaneously
told me that I was good at biting,
twigs, but since I moved into his
nest the man bites stealthily
when I am, for example,
recording my voice in
Kikar Milano, when I am,
for example, flying through
the park. These days the man
tells his little chicks to bite
anything they want, even
if I've asked him to save it
for the nightly repair. In fact,
he says now, for example,
have a string. Maggie
is saving it for the nightly
repair, or so she says. But that's
not until tonight. And by then
it will be too late for
spontaneity. In this nest,
says the man, we are spontaneous,
we are, he says, our most selfy
self. Maggie, he says, my pie,
aren't we our most selfy self?

GRANTED

You, said the wife to the husband, are taking me for granted. What, answered the husband, would you prefer to be taken for? In the husband's pocket were a wine opener, a business card, and a piece of lint. I should like very much to be taken, replied the wife, after combing through the lemons, for an impertinence. The husband looked at the wife. The husband took off his sunglasses to better see her pupils. No, no, said the wife. Now you are taking me for an aperture, and that is what got us into this dark place to begin with. To illustrate, she listed all the times that she, as an aperture, had had to illustrate. I did not realize, answered the husband, that an aperture was so dutiful. The husband walked twenty paces and sat down. He began carefully to persuade some waves into a harbor. Then he directed them to lap. Here, said the husband hopefully, is an incipient setting for an impertinence.

THE COST OF ART

Arik at the Jerusalem Print Workshop shows us something the cost of this month's mortgage payment. The cost of painting the walls in the two girls' bedrooms and the accent walls in the kitchen and on the staircase. The cost of my brand-new, full suspension mountain bike, which I cannot afford but, since the truck hit me, I need if I want to continue to share my man's fondest dreams. For the cost of two blood transfusions or half the cost of a caesarean section.

The print is like a blue whale in the blue sea, like rocks hidden in the waves, like a flag without a country. Its surface is scarred and scratched. It is a limited edition 1 of 12.

I had loved more this artist's black and white dandelion moon or her scratchy weather or her gossiping wheat, which takes three entire panels to finish its news, but my man says they are too dark for the wall. So we look only at the blue, sea-like, whale-like, mountain-like print with a flag without a country.

My friend Jane has bought giant paintings for half the price of the large leather sofa my man bought with his ex-wife and gave away when I moved in. For half the cost of the rug that he also bought with her that I'm making him sell.

We had come seeking a long, narrow painting to put on the staircase that joins our two floors, but though the space would fit the print Arik shows us, no one could see more than half the print at a time because of how the staircase slices back and forth.

To pay for a print that no one can see more than half of costs the same as half your new, top-quality refrigerator, I tell the man. He says I am the one paying for it, so I can do what I want. He says he's just telling me what he thinks. I tell him I agree with what he thinks.

After two years it was clear that if we didn't act, something would die. This is how a couple acts, he says. They get married. They bike mountains together. They buy art together. Why couldn't I just say thank you and be happy when someone offers me a home, he asks.

I do agree with what he thinks. That the shape of the wall is most fit for a long, narrow print that no one can see. But the shape of the eye is another thing.

This is a good example of fate, or physical attraction, or love—the meeting of two compatible dysfunctions. And it is why, after we pulled over the car yesterday on the way home to Tel Aviv from the print gallery because we were fighting so hard we could not pay attention to the road, we held each other all night, in sheets that cost 1/8 of the price of the print, and they are polished cotton sheets, 1,000 thread count that I bought severely discounted at Century 21 in New York the summer before I met the man.

We held each other all night. I stroked his face as if it were the stone in the print we hadn't yet decided to buy and slid my thigh between his thighs, like the hidden whale that I am absolutely certain is shaking its tail through the kelp in that blue print in the Jerusalem workshop, in its long metal tray in the gray cabinet, as the moon rises over the hills through the arched windows.

PERIODIC TABLE OF ELEMENTS

I have a chair said the woman to the man. It
is my chair I can sit on it. I can leave
it empty I can place it under the light
switch It can hold your jeans
or shorts or shirts after I have removed each
from my desk

I have a desk said the woman to the man
It is my desk Where will we put
your desk? the woman asked The man said
to the woman I do not need a desk
The man said I can use your desk But you cannot
said the woman, use my desk It is
my desk I need it. I
can buy you a different desk or the same desk
I can make you one just like it
No said the man I do
not need a desk We have
your desk No said the woman
to the man we do not
have my desk I
have my desk You
do not have at present a desk

The woman picked up the towel the man had placed
on the woman's desk This
the woman said to the man is not my towel

I have
towel
white
it is more
said the woman
it and dried it
initiative

I said
calmly
the woman
a towel
a new one
for the towel
for a towel
two hooks
and one
But not
The hook
to me
and a future
do not
Would you like
towel
No
at present
towel
It is fluffy

my towel
In my
Outside
gray
to the man
for me
But

thank you.
and pleasantly
said
You do not need
to fit
There is
in the bathroom
One hook is
hook is
for my current
is for a towel
but to a future
towel
presently
to go and buy
now, inquired
said the woman
a towel
I will use
It makes me

It is a white
imagination it is
of my imagination
Your son
he washed
on his own
thank you

I was
thanking you
I have
to buy me
on the hook
a hook
There are
for your towel
for my towel
towel
that belongs
me
which I
possess
your future
the man
I have
It is a nice
this towel
feel good

THE FAULT

One morning on her way the wife felt a little fault nipping at her ankle. She bent to the path through the dry grass and there it was, all alone and lost. Whose fault are you, little one, she asked, but the fault just began to cry. She stood there waiting, but no one came to claim it. So she picked it up. All day, through the city, in the library and classrooms, in the salary department and HR, among the crates of last-minute onions in the corner grocery store, no one had lost the fault, no one was looking for it. And when the husband met her at the bend she said I have found your fault. You dropped it on the way to the public.

No, no, said the husband. This isn't my fault. I am afraid it is yours. You must have dropped it when you were shaking out the tablecloths or else attempting to accidentally break the faux-crystal plastic pitcher my mother gave us for our beautiful new home. But as it was plastic, it only pretended to break. This is surely your fault. No, it is not my fault, said the wife. Perhaps it is your mother's fault; she might have left it with the faux-crystal plastic pitcher she bought for our beautiful new home. But it was not his mother's fault nor was it his father's fault, for his father had not brought with him his collection of faults when they had visited during the last minor holiday. They had not been accustomed to celebrating and had not even brought any pretend faults to parade. That is probably where it came from, said the woman. It fell out of step in the parade.

She felt sorry for the fault and decided to keep it. She wrapped it in her arms, fed the fault a little leftover fish from the too much she was said to have prepared. The fault found the fish delicious, and soon it was fast asleep in the bed that belonged to the husband and wife. The wife hoped it would sleep all night and not wake them up too early in the morning.

TOOLS

My parents teach me to take apart
car engines and reassemble them,
lying beneath them to coax fluids

(a roommate once changed her
own oil wearing white jeans and
a white silk blouse to prove a point)

or, palms open on the chassis,
fingering the wires, from above.
(Her mother was a food critic!)

When you lift a carburetor and carry it
to the workbench, it will not wrap
its legs around your hips—though

this is how mechanics are born.
Lined up along the walls like
playmates of the month are wrenches,

saws, clamps, screwdrivers, cases of bits,
hammers. One would be exciting enough,
as saws, for example, have teeth

but no eyes. They are the most
metaphorical of tools and the most
musical, the most cutting and persistent.

For once a saw has begun it is
nearly impossible for him to change
his mind about where he is, about

what he is about to do. The needle,
on the other hand, has an eye, and
the pinking shears are neither pink

nor sheer. Okay, I get it, said the child.
Next time I am eight years old, I'll
do it correctly. That was me.

The child of my parents is given
a jar of room temperature cream
to shake for twenty to thirty minutes

until nuggets of gold appear.
It is far easier on the muscles
than a churn. My parents are

proud of their prodigious idea.

3.

SUGAR FENCE MOON

Thee I grant sugar,
mine, and thee I grant three
moons, and thee I grant
a fence.

Fences make me feel mean; they always have. Cutting cows off from half of winter. And when the grass is finished growing over on the other side, then they'll get a big surprise! They can eat till they're so fat they'll be sold, and/or we can eat them, like trolls in the fairy tales.

Wire fences make me feel mean, reaching through wire fences to take the stunted mandarin oranges ripening too close to the fence line to be harvested, just before they begin to putrefy. Especially because my fists are just small enough, but almost too big, and I have to wiggle them a little when they are wrapped around mandarins. As if I were putting saltines in my purse in a diner, because in those kind of places, even if they serve you two packages with your soup and you do not eat them, they will not throw them away, but set them aside, and serve them to the next person. Although tortilla chips they do throw away, so you should probably put those into your purse, except they are not individually wrapped, and it can be messy.

Thinking about the Spam and Vienna sausages and salmon bones in the canned pink salmon, and pork and beans, and ranch style beans, and all the cans that opened unto me in my childhood is supposed to make me feel mean, the fact that I liked them, and with ketchup etc., but it doesn't. Metal cans do not make me feel mean, nor the things that came out of cans. Except for peas, which are disgusting. Especially when my grandmother sliced the Spam and fried it in eggs. But letting the mandarins rot and fall makes me feel mean. For they are not without beauty and thorns and hardship. They are full of seeds, so many seeds, even the French friends note their unusual flavor but say the seeds are too much. They flock, they flow, they descend as if a cosmic tableau, through the dark winter evening leaves, and you can squeeze their juice into a glass, and it is delicious.

No one says, princess, I'm glad you reminded me, take half my kingdom. No one says, here, have some money from my profits, have some votes. No one says, here, little stones, come flock around my head, and let the radiance from my face glow you up a little. And sometimes I do want that crown and that vote and that sunshine on my face.

Having too many moons makes me feel fat, though giving them my glow costs me nothing. I do not like the idea of them, the idea of things that want to reflect someone else's light.

My horoscope says it is because I feel sad when people want to take my sweetness for granted. I do not feel sweet today. I feel mean. I think of my second cousin, polishing the public steel statue of two sugar cubes in the town square in Dačice. My cousin would not have polished the statues, actually, for they are in the town square, and he is the groundskeeper of the palace. But it was in the palace of Dačice that the sugar cube was invented. And my second cousin cleans it up, like a faithful ant.

And I feel so mean, I am looking in my imagination at the cobwebs on the legs of the palace furniture instead of the frescos and chandeliers. Not the furniture in the public rooms, of course, for my second cousin is good at what he does, but at the broken piece in the warehouse.

For like him, when I was a child, I loved white bread with a hole cut in the middle and an egg fried inside— we never dared ask for it. It was one of those things one hoped for and was pleased with when it came. Or white bread with a circle of corn syrup on a plate, and we could dip the bread in it. And if there was extra syrup left, we'd lick the plate. It made us feel so rich to have it leftover. Not rich enough to waste it. But rich enough to lick the plate. Things like that, I will agree, only taste good if they are given to you. Not if you give them to yourself. But given by someone older than you on whom you are dependent, and in their honor, your little face glows with their reflected light.

THE RETROSPECT

One day the husband returned home and couldn't find his wife. When he'd left that morning she'd been standing before a retrospect she'd discovered in the pages of her diary. Although the print was largely illegible, the retrospect was shiny and alluring. Perhaps she'd gone wandering through the cabinets with the espresso pot again. But she wasn't among the frying pans nor pinging the beans. She wasn't duct-taping, or swimming in the laundry soap or turpentine, nor was she tapping nails or even hanging from the flowerpots on the balcony. Here I am, called the woman. Can't you see me? And then the husband noticed that next to the library, before the sliding glass, a luminous retrospect was silhouetting the hem of a woman's dress. But the woman wasn't there, which, in this particular retrospect, was probably for the best.

ON THE CLEANING
AND CARE OF RUGS

There were three threads that hovered
above the woman's head. How fortunate,
thought the woman. The threads waved
their thready threads, the threads did not
speak nor did they bother anyone. The
threads in fact were minding their own
business. It was the disaster who was
making a mess of the rug. It was a new
rug. In fact, it had been a flying carpet.
But when there is a disaster in the portico,
you may as well have used a regular rug
or even a rag. A flying carpet is useless,
and it is such a pity; the threads felt sorry
for the flying carpet. They colored, they
leapt. And the disaster sulked in the portico,
undecided about what to do next.

SPIDER

I do not want to
know I tell her what
my mother ate for lunch or
what she's rolling
in her crochet hooks what
it is like or what it is
that it is like
the neighbors stopped
to watch me pass
I passed on the sixth day
down the hall after I was
taught to lift one side
and slide out of bed.

She says Daddy says you
don't really know us as other
people do and we don't know
you I have just spent
a weekend with them we have just
spent four days together alone
in my hospital room. I learned
to roll over and slide
out of bed by myself it took
six attempts I have
learned to sleep an hour
at a time have learned
to not scream.

STEP MOTHER

Once I was a house, and the local delivery
boys couldn't stay away from my door,

the crack in my cleavage in need of repairing
to another room. My gardens luxurious and

fountains overflowed, etcetera.
When the baby came, it had all been so toothsome

and nail. Once I lived in a house in need of admiration
and repairs, and it suited me fine, my little inhabitant

of me and I decorated its dangling light bulbs
with flowers, the walls with circus sketches, the broken

jalousie we herbed and vined. The fixtures refused
fix. The sand spilled from the walls.

                              Now the houses
eat and eat, handfuls of money, bales of it, when I scoop
the feed barrel my coffee can scrapes bottom.

                              Yet every present
moment must be housed, and this one is no different.

Now I am carried, my baby with me, over the threshold of something
new. Suckle me up, present tense. We are throwing

the new house a party, so it will know who its mommy
and daddy are. Every night we ask did you brush your teethy

stairs, did you clean your little massive chin?
We wipe it down and sweep it up and grin. To be honest,

it's not even a house, but an apartment, but this isn't
about me and my judgments. Sometimes the house-

husband goes away for a few days, but he can never stay
away as long as he'd planned, for he's jealous

the little house will love its mommy more. Little house
did you lock? Did you do your housework? Have you

been fed, have you got a fresh dish of paint? One day
we played—have you grown?—battle on the white

countertop for the borders of the espresso pot. Of course,
the counter won the battle, and I lost the war, etcetera for if

I do not marry, I can just move out,

the house-husband said. We don't want to raise our house
like that. We must set a fine example. We mustn't confuse.

I am keeping so nicely the house in which I'm kept.
It isn't mine, but it is like mine, as long as I stay.

I am its step- and its stair-mother it is
adopted. I try to love it as much as if it were

mine, etcetera. And if I love it well enough, and
its house-husband, too, then one day it just might be,

till death do us part, as long as death parts me first. Little
house little house where have you been? The birds come

to call and the leaves of the trees gathering roots in
your alcoves are singing you lullabies that I will sweep

away in the morning.

THE VOICE

The woman often wondered what voice the girl
had when she was alone. Of course, it was possible
that the voice only sounded in company, and that
when the girl was alone, she did not actually exist
at all. No one had ever seen her alone. No one had
ever heard her speak when she was alone. The voice
was the voice of a toddler who had skipped her
morning nap. The voice was the voice of a girl who
did not exist except in the company of other bodies.
The voice was the voice of injustice, of a vague
and gentle fear, so soft and so comfortable, like
a sheet the girl might wrap around her if the girl
indeed were capable of existence inside of a cool,
soft sheet alone for five minutes in a room with
no one else around.

INALIENABLE

Life, liberty, and the pursuit of happiness. This is your inalienable right. *Inalienable* seems like a contradiction, as happiness is always alien, by definition.

But it is only the pursuit that is legally protected, that is not alien. Happiness itself is not within legal boundaries, set off, as it is, by a preposition.

Lovers of hunting / and beginners seeking your prey:/ don't aim your rifles/ at my happiness, says Taha Muhammad Ali, *which isn't worth/ the price of the bullet/ (you'd waste on it).*

And this inalienable right is applicable, according to the Constitution of the United States, only if a creator is witness, which brings in another alien force, which, when external to oneself, is not very conducive to happiness.

Although alien forces are excellent conductors.

ON THE POLISHING OF STONES

That's just what happens when you are an oppidum.
You suffer, said the woman to the oppidum. She herself

was sometimes fortified. And other times she served,
sometimes as an enclosure. But we, for whom sadness

is often the source of a blessed progress, could we exist
without them, she added? No, we could not. Hence

the invasions, hence the rapid stones and the beating bafflements,
the battles and the bats, the woman drew the water. The woman

tossed her fragments into the bath. The sun was setting
so fetchingly, one could almost pity the Vandals, pity the Goths

and Visigoths, for no one thought to remember that they, too,
once were children for whom a toothsome delight was joy enough

to fill an afternoon. Every lizard will have a dollop of sun
on its spread belly, and every child a drop of honey.

Here, for example, a treat or a treaty, here a truce.
The woman didn't have a treaty or a truce, a fig

or a tractor. All she had at her disposal was a grape
and a tomato, which, being round, were sufficient unto themselves

and also numerous, which was the pleasant thing
about being caught in the hail without a proper truce.

RAMPART

When the earth is supported by timber very much,
a tiny rampart is born.

The rivers were the best supporters of all the little ramparts
that joined to make oppida.

There is even a famous scandal in which two rivers loved
the same earth. There was heaval

and awashment, there was laundry and broken pots,
there were varieties of ambiguity,

several of them similar. But most of all it rained.
On rainy days the love was sloshy

and unsettled. One day the two rivers leapt across the land and fell
into each other. And that was the end

of the scandalous story about the rampant earth, its timberous
support, and the clanging bowls of onions

that had washed up on the left shore.

OFF THE BOAT, FALLEN

The designated boat rocker in our place of employment/domestic
arrangement/family of origin/graduate student housing apartment in
the Midwest in the 90s/hospital maternity ward

says rocking the boat is only fun if there is someone in the boat with
you.

The boat rocker's sea is delighted that though she is angry she is not
angry with him.

The boat rocker's sea is also upset /about his work/ he feels like a ser-
vant/and does not have the temperament //
    (the boat rocker has discussed this with various celestial bodies
    who agree the sea doesn't even like God to tell him what to do/
    much//less moons/sons/mermaids/suns/stars/his human sailors/
    captains//of certain high-tech companies /

    and now everyone is working at home so for the sea there are no
    more sunsets over the capital the office window overlooks / free
    lunches/ free shuttles to work// the sea says he likes it/ sea-ing at
    home (the boat rockers would like to ask if she can have his shut-
    tle/office window / free lunch and go to the sea's work place but he
    thinks she is joking).

The boat rocker has come to the conclusion that incompatible currents
create turbulent word banks.

Dear reader this is the boat rocker speaking /to say that when men sign their names to articles dismissing women who've won Nobel Prizes, and they've never read them / say in public if they weren't gay they'd date you/say they have no problem telling anyone/you're their boss (and Dear Sarah/ Dear Jane/I know Hilary lost to   ). What the hell do I expect will happen, eddy eddy eddy/ paddle   .

The boat rocker's copious faults have been told her (many times) and they are all true.

See the boat rocker cannot even contain herself and is already taking over all the narrative currents of this ravine/river/water park because she wants to make sure they are done properly/is up the river/out to sea/ my sincerest apologies

THE RING

Ire

The woman was often surprised by thank-yous for things she'd forgotten she'd done. Today she was given three different ones. She put them in the closet on the shelf above the snorkels.

Sometimes she was surprised by ire directed at her for things she'd forgotten she'd done. Both the ire and the thank you felt completely arbitrary. The same act could have inspired one person's thanks and another person's ire, since the acts were not done with any intent one way or another. Each was instinctive, and of similar quality, duration, content and form— the act that produced the ire and the act that produced thank you.

The reactions made her realize how she must appear to others, invisible, like the wind, sensed only in her movement through a room, and then, only sensed by the shape of the objects she touched, their behavior in response, their quality and character.

She obviously doesn't actually exist at all apart from the objects she daily caresses, it must have been an invisibility ring that he had placed on her finger that night. Unless the objects were immobile, or immutable, like God. Or especially if they were immobile and immutable, like God. It is difficult to tell what makes her real, and when and where, to whom, and for how long.

Clumsiness

The day after the ring the wife became clumsy.
The ring must weigh a great deal to throw off her
balance like that. The first morning after the ring she
poured a string of boiling coffee across her fingers, and
three weeks later they are still bandaged. Two days
after the ring she broke a plate. Three days after the
ring, she lifted a crystal decanter to put it away and it
dropped on her head, where it made a large lump, and
fell to the sink where it broke a triangle piece of
porcelain clear off. It had been a crystal decanter that
the man had received as a gift from his first marriage,
and he had asked the woman if they could keep it. The
woman wondered how many objects in the man's house
had joined the pact to kill her. After that she rested for a
day from getting hurt. On day four she cut her finger on
a new knife, and on day five she broke a wine glass.
There are so many objects in this large house, she felt
she would never be done.

Bed

Ever to go to bed angry
is a very bad thing, the wife

knows. Maybe that's why since

the ring she cannot bear
to sleep in the bed. It might

be the bed, is she a princess? But
it also might be that his child

-ren never go to bed. It might
have nothing to do with the bed

but with the pecking order.
Every time she orders a peck,

it tickles itself away
from the original sense.

It ends up biting her hand. Once
she asked him to go without her

to the sea and to take the children
so she could work; he did.

That night she tried to sleep in
the bed. She did come to the bed

in the middle of the night, and he did
throw his arms around her waist,

and in the morning
from work he texted her a kiss.

But somewhere in between the sheets
of the road that takes him to and from work,

and the screens of the laptop, the phone,
the television that follow his daughter

all day and all night before which
the wife must pass back and forth,

the kiss got lost. She imagines
it stopped to look at the screen,

too, and never pulled itself
away, or it falls into sleep

when the screen goes dark,
and it grows dark

far away from the bed.

The Ring

Whenever the woman
catches sight

of the ring
on the hand

across her abdomen
in the elevator's

particularly unflattering
mirror the woman

suddenly understands
the mystery she's

teasing:
that the ring

is what has
been doing all

the work these
days—gravity,

hydroponics, bed
making, bills.

She's hardly
had to think

at all, all she has
to do right

now is hold
her breathing

in its place and keep
her finger

in the circle
created by the ring.

4.

WAGES, WOMEN, AND IMMIGRANTS

On the day the American troops stationed on the Mexican border began firing tear gas and rubber bullets at migrants seeking asylum in America in January 2019, my sister-in-law's Facebook post was how to make a taco salad. My mother's fb post was a video called "teach children to be kind" in which a blond boy whose lunch box is empty goes out during break to drink water, and when he returns he discovers all of his classmates have filled his empty box with one or two items from their own boxes.

My earliest memory of my mother's political engagement was her opposition to the National Organization of Women around 1982, when the Equal Rights Ammendment was defeated. I remember my mother being opposed to the ERA. I suppose there are things you could fault NOW for, but I remember being puzzled over her opposition to the ERA.

> Section 1. No political, civil, or legal disabilities or inequalities on account of sex or on account of marriage, unless applying equally to both sexes, shall exist within the United States or any territory subject to the jurisdiction thereof.

> Section 2. Congress shall have power to enforce this article by appropriate legislation

F has pointed out that my parents are not wage earners—as a rice farmer/rancher family, we were almost completely self-sufficient. My father taught me to drive a tractor and take apart and put together a car engine before I learned to drive at fifteen, and my mother taught my brothers to vacuum and scrub the toilets; we produced our own vegetables, meat, milk, eggs; my mother sewed our clothes. My mother had no use for the ERA, but she was concerned that women would be drafted during war. Somewhere in there must have been a statement about abortion.

Sometimes she amazed me. When I moved to Philadelphia and was shocked by the poverty, the school districts that had no textbooks, chairs, or Xerox machines in the after-school programs I worked with, my mom commented, "If everyone who had a baby had to put it in a national lottery, and it could end up anywhere, I bet they'd clean up the inner cities pretty quickly."

My mother was against the Women's March after the 2016 election. She said she resented "being made to feel guilty."

The first time either she or my father worked for wages, they worked for minimum wage—and she was not allowed to sit down during lulls in sales at the Prasek's Smokehouse gift shop on Highway 59. She was very popular there, because she took such an interest in cancer cases, and many of the patrons were on their way to MD Anderson. She even began a prayer journal, recording the illnesses of those who'd stopped for a kolache or a pig-in-the blanket, and promising to pray for them. She became a draw.

My father had just lost our farm, after the 1996 Farm Bill snuck into the Welfare Reform Bill, then 9/11 made oil prices skyrocket for two years, and he'd not budgeted for that. Unfortunately, in 2000 my father had just used his savings to double the size of the farm—we'd always leased land before. Then there were three years of drought, and then he got colon cancer. So we had to sell the farm.

During my father's illness, my mother would sob that she was so afraid he'd die. My sister and I would tell her how much we loved her and say we couldn't imagine how it must feel—they'd been together since they were fifteen and seventeen; married since they were eighteen and twenty. "And then if he died," my mother had added, "I'd have to get a job!" But then again, she had voted against the ERA, and it still has not been ratified.

On the other hand, she protested the death penalty the year *Dead Man Walking* came out. And when we were in high school, because my aunt who was a nun lived in the Casa Juan Diego Catholic Worker house, we helped illegal immigrants get fake social security cards, and when my dad hired one to work for him on the farm, I gave him a Spanish-English dictionary for his birthday, and he paid the worker minimum wage. We were so proud of him then.

WEDDING GIFT

The print that began the ending of my marriage was so
gorgeous, I'd forgotten how gorgeous it was in real life, laid
out on the examination table, as the framer and I took measure
of what lay before us—the paper itself and the textures, alive
and breathing. The whale inside it shook a bit and swished,
but it might have been the waves brushing against a stone, or
it might not have been water at all, just strange birds in the
Negev against a blue and white sky about to blink off without
the fanfare of sunset. Tears burst when my fingertips brushed
it. The framer, also, cleared his throat upon sliding it from
its canister and unfolding it across the table. He touched the
ragged edges and caressed the signature—print 1 of 12, he
whispered. Every time he touched it he asked permission, as
if we were lovers—may I remove it from its box? May I spread
it out? The framer is going to Monte Negro for a week, so
he'll have it ready on Friday, Sept. 20. Once home, I undress
and wait in bed, the sheets and covers indeterminate colors of
green, for the dream to return to the point it left off, the last
time I touched it. Then I was swimming all night through
the air/sand/water that was the page of the print, and while
nothing in particular happened, it was the nothing particular
that happens when you walk on a strange and beautiful
landscape for the first time. Or the nothing particular that
ends a marriage. Then every leaf and every water drop and
every strange flower is a happening.

F TAKES A FENCE

What on earth, inquired the wife, are you going to do with another fence?

I can't yet say, said the husband, but how could I not take it? It was just lying there, he added, on the table, next to the butter knife and the idea of Russian braids. But husband, persisted the wife, where are you going to keep it? The cupboards are full of fences you've taken, we have no more room on the wall, and even the pillows are stuffed, she added, with fences. Not to mention the duvet. The husband looked pensive, and then he looked perspicacious, and then he looked like a man who has once remembered a dream.

The wife waited next to the fence the husband was taking next to the butter knife and the idea of Russian braids, and also next to the swirly blue napkins while the sun set and then rose, and the climate took on a fetching languor, so that soon all the fences were dropping their pickets. And far, far away a little sun seed was seething in the sea. In the morning, the husband fingered a fallen picket. What would you think, he inquired of the wife, if instead of a fence, I collected pickets? The wife took the picket to the mossy light, itching to pick her teeth.

TOOTH

One day a tooth was found where it oughtn't have been. It was
old. It was older than any other tooth that has ever been found,
it was so old there were not even tooth faeries yet, or else

there were only tooth faeries. Tooth faeries and Neanderthals.
This person tooth, this *Homo sapiens* tooth, arrived eight thousand
years earlier than the person to whom it belonged. Or else

that person was eight thousand years earlier than was expected.
For Neanderthals, though smarter than we think, were not as smart
as *Homo sapiens*. Probably they were more emotional, less

rational, more superstitious. For example, they believed in faeries,
which they called gods. On the other hand, they developed a stone-
tool industry, made fire, built cave hearths (although apparently

they had to compete with bears), played around with adhesive
birch-bark tar, were crafty with clothes, blankets, ponchos, for they
could weave, go faring through the Mediterranean, use medicinal

plants. Which was a good thing, for they often injured themselves
severely. They lived in a high-stress environment. With lots of
Homo sapiens (and bears). My child still asks me to perform

exorcisms, and we lead the bears out of her closet at night. Some
times we pray to them and stroke our thigh bones. We also liked
to adorn ourselves. Why not? *Homo sapiens* couldn't have been

easy to live with. Obviously, the Neanderthals stored food and
roasted, boiled, and smoked, and do to this day—I grew up, for
example, with a smokehouse, but we are not very smart, and once

we forgot to bank it well, and the fire burned a hole through
the pine floor, and the meat stank a little that winter. I mean *Homo
sapiens* are not as violent as bears, probably passive-aggressive,

perhaps rational, as their name suggests, but o my dear tooth-faery-
god, so priggish, and the earliest confirmed arrival of *Homo sapiens* in
Europe showed Neanderthals somehow shared

the land for thousands of years. So, it is possible. Everyone likes to call
them "big-boned," or "healthy." Look, you don't have to tell me about
thunder thighs. But some men like thighs like that.

Even though the *Homo sapiens* ate all the yogurt and cheese
in the house, took the best meat. The Neanderthals could talk,
of course they could, but they just couldn't express their needs

in a way that *Homo sapiens* could accept. They didn't know
the Socratic method. They preferred to make music. On bear bones
—the thigh bones, to be specific—they collected unusual objects,

which is what F calls mine, and asks why don't we throw them
out? So why *did* the Neanderthals die out, if we were capable
of copying the technologies of the new arrivals?

Some scientist called Klein is asking. Klein has obviously never
lived with a bunch of *Homo sapiens* who overran his house.
If you ask me, he has probably never lived at all.

I think Neanderthals probably slipped into a cave
painting because we know magic,
to wait the *Homo sapiens* out.

NAMING THE ANIMALS

Shopping on Friday F tells his wife about the animals. There is a mouse that's made a nest in the sea chest where he keeps the rum. And a rat that is chewing the feet of the furniture. He forgets its name. It is a rat or a mouse, he feels very certain, and there is a roach in the bathroom. Well, it isn't in the bathroom, it is at the foot of his wardrobe, but his wardrobe is near the bathroom. If he sees it again, he will spray. There are gecko stars upon the screen but those are just their feet, not really stars, and guinea pigs in the garden, but we knew that before. On Sunday F enters the bathroom, poison bottle in hand. But the only thing in the bathroom is his wife, who looks up from the mirror. On her fingertip is a long thin whisker, or possibly a hair.

F AND THE VIOLINS

You animal, F carefully proclaimed one early afternoon,
while the roses were climbing the fence and breathing
the little leaves below them. The little leaves below
them rustled, *you understand*, above them birds were leaving their
brown wing prints all over the freshly washed sky, *only violins*. M
would have to tell the sky cleaner
to use more timely erasers next time.

Why do you say that? M inquired. *Is it the brown wing prints over the
freshly washed sky? Is it the star prints on the window? The sky cleaner
is coming tomorrow, don't worry.*

But it was not the wing prints and it was not the star prints. It was the
sky cleaner herself. *But F*, said M, carefully rubbing out F's mark from
the celestial sphere that was beginning to roll down the hall, *I fed the
sky cleaner myself from my own bread and butter. I did not take your
bread nor your butter, not even the butter you left on the knife nor the
crumbs that fell from your chin fur.*

Yes, F said, *but you brought her here into my common air, and I
explicitly forbade it.*

And it was true, M had invited the sky cleaner into F's common air
after F had explicitly forbidden it. For weeks they had done without the
sky cleaner, ever since the sky cleaner had slipped M some pity. And F
thought that pity was bad for M's figure. In fact, M had been growing
quite fat on the sky cleaner's pity.

But it's also true that F complained each day from 4 p.m. to 6 p.m. that M had left too many stars scattered around, and cloud dust, and that he'd not liked her erasers. *You couldn't concentrate on the melody with all the stars*, M said.

M, F said, *it doesn't matter. You do not understand, and so though I am loathe to do so, I must now resort to violins.* M said nothing, and F continued,

You will agree it is not my fault, it is your fault, because you do not understand. M sat still and the bird wings paused, and the roses faded into their white background, the rustling quieted so as to hear the violins.

AND THE VIOLINS

Sometimes M felt herself drawn to the celestial music the sky
cleaner's bright cloth made as it rubbed the window glass. Along
the garden wall, the cracks stilled and, indeed, all the lines began
to wither, the roots and the seeds and the nets and the bonds, the
white space grew wider and wider, and M felt herself begin to
slip. She flailed and found herself in the grip of an eraser—for she
was spelling violence incorrectly. On the other end was a pencil
lead. M led the lead to the bottom and drew herself a floor. Later
F would say, contemplating the floor M had drawn, that in fact,
he hadn't meant that kind of violins.

AND THE VIOLINS

M had been falling a long, long time past the desert bowls and the buttered knives past the lines of ants across the balcony past the night sheep pinned for counting past the pots and their chubby spoons she fell and she fell and she fell and she fell she wasn't sure she would ever stop falling.

THE GARDEN

First the wife would pull up the weeds in the garden,
then harvest the tomatoes, lettuce, grapes, lemons,
oranges, eggplant, artichoke, etc. while the husband
would walk to the grocer and buy tomatoes, lettuce grapes,
lemons, oranges, eggplant, artichoke, etc. for whatever was in
season in the garden was also in season in the shops. The husband bought them on sale.

Of course, if the tomatoes and lettuce, grapes, lemons, oranges,
eggplant, artichoke, etc. from the garden would taste as good as
the ones in the shop, the husband said he would kindly eat the
garden ones instead. The wife could note, for example, that her
zucchini were great, so the husband never was obligated to buy
those on sale in the shops during their time in the garden. The
husband and the wife lived together and ate together from one
or many large pots. For just because the wife had grown tomatoes and lettuce grapes, lemons, oranges, eggplant, artichoke,
etc., did that mean the husband was never allowed to buy them?

AND THE GARDEN

Tunneling out from the weeds in the garden, the wife does, in fact, feel like a small animal. It is true she is small and sharp, and her hands and feet are wet with stars, but the wife actually doesn't like to gnaw; thinking of wood between her molars nauseates her, in fact. Even chewing is laborious. She prefers to use her tongue. Also, she prefers living stalks to dead wood and the higher branches to the lower. Sometimes the wife wanders through the house looking for the book from which the husband received his education in taxonomy. It might have been a question of spelling, except that the wife knows most of the spells. She has pulled up several trees during the span of their common life, but for those she has used her fingers, not her teeth.

Nevertheless, it is true that the husband's furniture is thoroughly gnawed. The feet especially.

THE BOAT ROCKER'S POSTSCRIPT

The bright dark red lipstick supplies the ballast. The boat rocker feels the pull. It is I, of course, not the oars, not the current, not the surprisingly expensive lipstick that is the oars, the current, the very paint on the boat of the lips, who is speaking. I want to say that I am tired.

I would like very much one day to be the dragonfly with transparent wings posed on the oarlocks, the rim of the boat, the leaves that are dipping as I speak, over the currents that I can only guess at. I do not know what lies below this boat, what sunken radiance, what rusted dreams hidden in their leaky boxes, what fish with hook scars in their mouths, what bodies bloated with water, resting on the floor.

The lipstick is Chanel. In real life it looks ridiculous on my grandmother's upper lip which now I wear. I have scarred it by fainting one night and hitting my mouth on the edge of a desk. When the toddler woke up for gan it was too late for stitching my lip whole. But on camera, the color is divine. The waves will not take me as long as I am wearing it. How I really feel is how anyone really feels in any circumstance. I am longing, as you are, for someone to say, I like you.

You are doing great. Look at you, sitting here with your calloused hands, noting the sparkle of the water, the passing of the days. Each one is a bubble of time, which I would gladly pop with you.

THE SPIDER

Yesterday I cried until there was no yogurt left
until all my mother's cabbages rolled out
of the hallway closet, until the river crouched
into a green pool and blinked, I cried
until the too much order signaled its disorder
until a box filled with little bars of soap
appeared until the spider finished rolling
up its white package of meat in the garden
until the neighbor's barbecue pits were
loaded up onto the back of the truck and
the children popped up like mushrooms
though clearly there had been no rain.

STORYBOARD

We are sitting in the room describing the symbols, you do not call them symbols, of course, you call them the children, you call them kashrut—*bless you* I want to say in between dashes—the symbols all point in one unambiguous direction. I am standing between the pointing symbols and the targets at which they are aimed.

In this story I am the bad witch of the west, the evil stepmother, the siren, that kind of thing, this is just a mock-up, we can work out the details later, in this story I make everyone feel like shit. The less I appear in the story the bigger I grow I do not like it here in this particular story and the other characters resent it when I try to escape into the double space between each full stop and the double spaces between paragraphs or the single spaces between words. I have tried them all. I should have been using sans serif here because they are always catching me by the serif and pulling me back in. Without me the words would have no spaces and nothing would make sense.

NO MORE FUN/HOUSE

Diana's left our service/and the sink
is full of fresh clouds after the rain / we hung
onto the breakfast melons and their melancholy/
strolled to the shores of the teacup/ sat
and watched the waves repeated / rush
to the harbor slam themselves and shatter
rise and fall, like a glass held by an unsteady
god/ at the end of love/ it isn't love undoing my life
undoing the more we are/apart
the less I will / back

--

one can't unspill
no one can/the source
so self-ful it cannot lie/cannot
even/speak/can stand/
it/when it can't it spills
nevertheless the events
here/such/as they/are are
narrated back/
wards because hind/sight/is
topical/ one means, I do/it
depends on the site
it's difficult/to hitch
the narrative/sequence
some parts wonder/out
of turn/undermining what
I've been/trying to compose
myself for a long
/run or the long
or time

--

I have come to this
place a quiet/accident
this little borrow /cool dark
bed in /the corner I have
spent fifteen minute-hands
hand-watering the petunias
pinching / off the dead
blooms. I planted them/more soil
weeding / out the hours. They turn
their faces / to me. I am
a tiny deity / to them
I am the rain—not the sun
or the air, not earth/ just
the rain. I thank them they
thank me. None
of them trembles/ before me,
mistaking me for storm.

--